Miriam's Cup
A PASSOVER STORY

BY FRAN MANUSHKIN

ILLUSTRATED BY BOB DACEY

SCHOLASTIC INC.

New York Toronto London Auckland Sydney
Mexico City New Delhi Hong Kong Buenos Aires

For my singing and dancing congregation, B'nai Jeshurun, especially Rabbi J. Rolando Matalon, Rabbi Marcelo R. Bronstein, and Music Director, Ari Priven; and for my Seder Sisters: Denyse Dolny-Lipsy, Claire Hertz, Nina Kaufman, Trudi Levine, and Zelda Weiss; for Eileen Schmidman; for Elizabeth Stabler; and finally, for my editor, Dianne Hess, a true Woman of Valor!

— F. M.

To my mother,

Terri Gurganious

— B. D.

Special thanks to Josh Lesser, Rabbinic Intern at Congregation Beth Simchat Torah and Rabbi Melinda Panken from Temple Shaaray Tefila for their invaluable help in fact-checking the manuscript.

ISBN 0-439-81111-2
Text copyright © 1998 by Fran Manushkin
Illustrations copyright © 1998 by Bob Dacey

Music on inside back cover: excerpted from "Miriam's Song" from AND YOU SHALL BE A BLESSING recording. Music and lyrics by Debbie Friedman. Lyrics (based on Exodus 15:20-21) copyright © 1988 by Deborah Lynn Friedman (ASCAP). Published by Sounds Write Productions, Inc. (ASCAP).

12 11 10 9 8 7 6 5 4 3 2 1   6 7/0

Printed in the U.S.A.   40

First Bookshelf edition, February 2006

The text type was set in Aries.
Bob Dacey's art was rendered in watercolors.
Papyrus, a kind of paper used by the ancient Egyptians, appears as a background for the text throughout this book.
Cover art © 1998 by Bob Dacey
Book design by Kristina Albertson

EVERY SPRING, Passover arrives with a tumult and flurry — such a clanging of pots and a sweeping of rooms! In cities and towns all over the world, many a house is turned upside down.

At the Pinsky home, Miriam and her brother Elijah always help with the preparations. Every year, before the Seder, Papa reminds Elijah, "Don't forget to polish Elijah's cup."

Elijah never forgets. He's so proud to be named after the great prophet.

Well, *this* year, Mama had a surprise for Miriam. She gave her a box wrapped in paper as golden as sunlight. "Before you open your gift," Mama said, "I want to tell you about Miriam, the prophet you are named for."

"This is no time for a story!" Papa groaned. "Our guests will be here soon."

"*This* story cannot wait," Mama insisted, and here is how she began....

EVERY PASSOVER we tell the story of
how God freed our ancestors from slavery.
Well, one of these ancestors was a brave and
clever girl named Miriam. She lived in Egypt
with her mother and father, and her brother
Aaron. And, oh, their lives were so hard!

In those days, the Egyptian pharaoh forced
the Israelites to make bricks for his cities. Each
night, Miriam's father, Amram, came home so
caked with mud she could hardly recognize
him. Miriam would bring her papa warm water
to wash the mud away, and sing him soothing
songs. Miriam dearly loved to sing, for it was
her way of praising God.

One day the cruel pharaoh decided there were too many Israelite slaves. He feared that someday they would rise up against him. So he decreed that all their boy babies be drowned in the river!

When Miriam's father heard this, he told his wife, Jocheved, "We must divorce each other. Then we will have no more sons for Pharaoh to kill." And so, Miriam's parents parted. The other Israelite men followed Amram's lead, and they divorced their wives, too.

"Papa," Miriam said boldly, "your action is worse than Pharaoh's. He wants to kill boys, but you are declaring no girls will be born, either."

"That is true," agreed Amram sadly.

"You are a good person," Miriam said in a strong voice. "God will honor your decrees and punish those who would harm you. Papa, you must remarry Mama. She is going to give birth to a child who will set our people free."

Although Miriam was only six years old, her words impressed her father so much that he *did* remarry her mother. All the other slaves followed his lead, and they remarried, too.

How joyfully Miriam danced around her parents' wedding canopy, singing songs to the bride and groom!

Many months later, a baby boy was born.
And the house filled with radiant light! Amram
kissed his daughter and said, "Miriam, your
prophecy is coming true."

But Miriam's mother, Jocheved, knew the
child's life was in danger, for Pharaoh was still
drowning every Israelite boy baby.

"I will place my son in the Nile as Pharaoh
ordered," she decided, "but he shall not
drown!" She wove a sturdy ark to hold him,
and placed it in the bulrushes where Pharaoh's
daughter came to bathe. "She has a kind face,"
Jocheved said. "Surely she will not let him
drown."

"I will watch over my brother," Miriam
promised, as she hid herself behind the tall
reeds.

Soon enough, the princess came to bathe, and God chose that moment to make the child cry. The princess took pity on him and said, "I know you are a Hebrew child, but I will not let you die as my father decreed. I will raise you as my son, but I need a Hebrew nursemaid to feed you."

"I can find you a nursemaid!" called Miriam, rushing out of her hiding place. And she brought back her own mother!

"Miriam," Jocheved whispered, cradling her son once more. "You are a true blessing to us."

The pharaoh's daughter named the baby Moses, and raised him in great comfort inside the palace. Meanwhile, Moses' sister Miriam and his brother Aaron grew up amid great suffering, toiling in the fields and sleeping on the hard, stony ground.

One day, Moses came upon an Egyptian overseer beating a Hebrew slave. While trying to protect the slave, Moses killed the overseer. This so angered Pharaoh that he ordered Moses' death. And so Moses fled from Egypt — for forty years!

Still, Miriam never lost her faith in God, and she kept everyone's spirits up with her joyful songs. "I know God is watching over us," Miriam sang.

And she was right. God *did* see how the people suffered. And God told Moses, "Go back to Egypt and tell Pharaoh to let my people go!"

Moses did as God ordered, but Pharaoh sneered at Moses. "*I* am God here, and I will do no such thing."

On that day, God sent down the first plague, turning the Nile River to blood. Oh, how it stank of dying fish! But Pharaoh still refused to let the Israelites go.

So God sent down more plagues.

Thousands of frogs filled the Egyptians' beds and feeding bowls.

Lice and wild beasts afflicted them. And pestilence!

Boils covered their bodies, and hail pounded down from the sky.

Still, Pharaoh would not let the Israelites go.

Then God sent the most terrible plague of all: every first born of the Egyptians was slain. The Israelites did not die, for God ordered them to mark their doorposts and lintels with blood. The Angel of Death saw these marks and knew to pass over their homes.

Finally, Pharaoh understood the power of God. He told Moses, "Take your people away this night." The Israelites were forced to leave so quickly their bread dough had no time to rise — so they carried it in kneading bowls on their shoulders.

"We must take our drums, too," Miriam told the women. "God is performing miracles for us. Let us give thanks with our joyful songs."

That night, the Jewish people began their journey out of slavery. Thousands of families marched in a long line, stopping only when they reached the shore of the Red Sea.

Suddenly, over the rush of the waves, they heard the sound of thundering hooves. "Pharaoh has changed his mind!" the people cried. "He is sending his soldiers to kill us!"

Quickly, God commanded Moses, "Raise your staff over the water!"

Moses obeyed, and God made the waters rise up and part. Two shining walls of water formed, making the seabed a dry path to walk on.

The Israelites hurried across.

"Pursue them!" Pharaoh ordered his soldiers, and the soldiers drove their chariots into the sea.

As soon as the Israelites were safely on the other shore, God told Moses, "Raise your staff again." When he did, God brought the waters crashing down, and Pharaoh's army was drowned.

As the Israelites witnessed God's awesome power, they declared, "We must sing God a song of gratitude." Moses led the men in song, and Miriam led the women. She sang:

Sing to God, for God is high.
The horse and rider God has cast into the sea.

In praise of God, Miriam and the women danced, filling the air with the sound of their timbrels and drums.

"Our people are free," Miriam's father told her. "Your great prophecy has come true."

Every year at Passover, we tell this story of our deliverance. As we remember our ancestors, we should also remember Miriam's faith and courage: how she convinced her father to remarry her mother, how she watched over Moses in the bulrushes, and how she led all the women as they sang the *Song of the Sea*.

Indeed, God remembered Miriam. In her honor, God created a well of clear spring water. Before the Israelites entered the promised land, they wandered in the desert for forty years. And wherever Miriam went, her well would follow!

When the people were parched with thirst, they had only to raise their staffs and chant: "Spring up, o well!" And the water gushed forth, shooting up high as pillars!

The sweet, fresh water sustained their lives. Oh, never was there such a wondrous well!

"AND SO," concluded Mama, "that is how your namesake, Miriam the prophet, played her part in the great Passover story."

Little Miriam smiled with pleasure. "Where is Miriam's well now?"

"In Israel, where else?" Mama said. "Now you may open your gift."

The family gathered around the table as Miriam untied the ribbon and opened the box. Inside she found a sparkling crystal goblet. "This is Miriam's cup," said Mama. "Every year we will place it on our Passover table so we may honor her."

As Miriam filled the goblet with water, Papa told Mama, "That *is* an important story. I'm glad you told it."

During the Seder, everyone sang a song about the prophet Miriam. As they sang, Miriam Pinsky gazed at Miriam's cup, hoping the prophet would come and sip some water.

It is very likely that she did, for the brave and joyful spirit of the prophet Miriam is surely at every Seder!

AUTHOR'S NOTE

The Passover holiday lasts for eight days and eight nights. On the first and second nights, families and friends gather together to hold the ceremonial dinner and service, called the "Seder." During the Seder, the participants reenact the drama of the Israelites' exodus from Egypt, their flight from slavery to freedom.

The guide for the Seder is a book called the *Haggadah*, which means "the telling." Its main narrative comes from the book of Exodus. The *Haggadah* also includes prayers, songs — and *Midrashim*, which are explanations of the symbols and meaning behind the biblical text. For thousands of years, rabbis and scholars have sought to fill "gaps" in the Bible with midrashic commentary and story. In this way, *Midrashim* can clarify and enrich our understanding of biblical people and events. Some of the events of Miriam's life we know from what we are told in the Bible. Other events of her life we know from various *Midrashim* and *Aggadot* (legend). *Miriam's Cup: A Passover Story*, is based on the Bible, *Midrashim*, and *Aggadot*.

As with the Pinsky family in the story, many people today celebrate Miriam by including a cup for her on their Seder table to be placed alongside the other important ritual objects. Any available glass, cup, pitcher, chalice, or vessel can be used as Miriam's cup. Or it can be handmade from any material, and decorated with personal objects, such as family jewelry, shells, bells, flowers, photographs — anything to add to the meaning and intimacy of the ritual. The cup is filled with water, as Miriam is always associated with water. By displaying a visible symbol of the great prophet, we can honor her for the role she played in the Israelites' exodus. Miriam is also associated with song and dance, and at many Seders, participants sing songs about her and dance with drums and tambourines. Debbie Friedman's powerful song, excerpted on the back of this book, is one of the most popular songs about Miriam; it will make everyone want to get up and dance!

As we remember Miriam, it is also good to recall the heroism of two other Hebrew midwives, Shifra and Puah, who, at the risk of their own lives, defied Pharaoh's orders to drown all the Hebrew children. Their refusal is history's first recorded case of civil disobedience in defense of a moral cause. In the Jewish tradition, Pharaoh's daughter is also honored as one of ten people to ascend to heaven while still alive.

I hope this book will pass along to readers a joyous new ritual for the Seder, and that it will add to our collective appreciation of the many biblical women who have enriched the Jewish tradition.

BIBLIOGRAPHY

My story of the prophet Miriam is based on several Midrashim *as well as* Aggadot—*legends and stories. My chief sources are:*

Culi, Rabbi Yaakov, *The Torah Anthology*, Meam Lo-Ez, Book 4, Israel in Egypt, (translated by Rabbi Aryeh Kaplan), Maznaim Publishing Corporation, New York, 1978.

Culi, Rabbi Yaakov, *The Torah Anthology*, Meam Lo-Ez, Book 5, The Redemption, (translated by Rabbi Aryeh Kaplan), Maznaim Publishing Corporation, New York, 1979.

Ginzberg, Louis, *Legends of the Jews*, Vol. 1-6, (translated by Henrietta Szold and Paul Radin), The Jewish Publication Society of America, Philadelphia, 1909-1956.

Steinsaltz, Adin, *Biblical Images: Men and Women of the Book*, Basic Books, New York, 1984.

The Torah: A Modern Commentary, Exodus 2: 4-8, 15; 20-21; Numbers 20: 1-2; Micah 6: 4, (edited by W. Gunther Plaut), Union of American Hebrew Congregations, New York, 1981.